THE ILLITERATE

ÁGOTA KRISTÓF

The Illiterate

translated from the French by Nina Bogin
introduction by Helen Oyeyemi
afterword by Gabriel Josipovici

A NEW DIRECTIONS
PAPERBOOK ORIGINAL

Manufactured in the United States of America
First published as New Directions Paperbook 1559 in 2023
Design by Erik Rieselbach

Library of Congress Control Number: 2022057398

10 9 8 7 6 5 4 3 2 1

New Directions Books are published for James Laughlin
by New Directions Publishing Corporation
80 Eighth Avenue, New York 10011

CONTENTS

INTRODUCTION

It's a triumph over probability that Ágota Kristóf's *The Illiterate*, first published in French in 2004, is available for perusal at all. In a 1999 interview, this unparalleled writer's answer to the question "What are you working on at the moment?" indicated that she was barely writing anymore—oh, if only it were possible to hear the author's tone as she told Gergely Nagy: *Somehow I've gone off literature.*[1]

At some point between 1999 and 2006, the withdrawal from written narrative crystalized, and in 2011 the author elaborated on the situation. She remarked—in a way that makes it possible to glimpse her skipping the part of the writing process where the thoughts are committed to the page, a static medium of page which only accepts familiar phrases, and moving on to the new chapters that can only be written within the far greater flexibilities of the mind—that *I have the whole thing in my head, I basically have it written. It is very easy to write it down when it is already there in my head. Then I wrote a few pages, but I kept repeating what I had already written. I started again, then I wrote the end, several times, but then I left it off.*[2]

And yet . . . here, through the gaps in a growing aversion to telling tales, *The Illiterate* speaks. We hear something of Kristóf's view of literature, and the paths along which she brings her own contributions to it. Read on a certain level, this appears to be the story of a Hungarian with anti-Communist sympathies who, having journeyed into bitter exile in 1956,[3] found herself sorely pressed by the necessity of decoding an environment that forced her sense of self into strange new shapes. When it came time to write about—and against—these distorting experiences, Kristóf didn't turn to her mother tongue. The notion of a language with words forming so complete a synergy with her conception of her surroundings that *I couldn't imagine that another language could exist, that a human being could pronounce a word that I wouldn't be able to understand*—this was no longer a livable reality. Instead there was a job at the Swiss watch factory, manufacturing time in silence,[4] and there was the emergence of a persona perceived not only as vulnerable, but pitiable. Kristóf's narrator doesn't mention any unkind acts aimed at her group of refugees, but some of the kindnesses described cloud the heart with unease: *On Sunday, after the soccer game, the spectators come to look at us through the barracks fence. They offer us chocolate and oranges, naturally, but also cigarettes and even money. It no longer reminds us of concentration camps, but of a zoo.*

We're informed that five years pass, during which the émigré acquires spoken French, but can't read the words. Since a reader must either read or lose everything, written French is the linguistic modality that the narrator of *The Illiterate* must learn to understand her new world despite the marrow-chilling absence of obligation on the part of written French (or of any written language) to understand her. The prose of Kristóf's published books, written in French, and in a style that is frequently deemed "minimalistic," stems from her preferring to exclude *adjectives and things that are not real, that have their origin in feelings* and from the difficulty of trusting one's footing when dealing with phrases that defy perfection.[5] Kristóf's writing (and a great deal of the reading that she loved—Victor Hugo, Rosseau, Voltaire, Sartre, Camus, Michaux, Francis Ponge, Sade) was done in a vocabulary with which she was at war at all times. In giving the writerly aspects of herself over to French, Kristóf surrendered her linguistic capabilities to catastrophic loss: *This language is killing my mother tongue.* Winding the thorny thread of this loss around her pen, visceral dread, swiftly flashing sensations of release and all, the way of this Illiterate is rebellion. That's one reading of Kristóf's eloquent brevity. We could stop there: sentences hurled with perfect aim at the border between one language and another is quite enough to be going on with as a writer's life's work. But Kristóf's rebel vocabulary does still more; it *is* more. Think of the various ways in which verbal ornaments act as a veil, suggesting (or negotiating a perception of) fluency. Encountering Kristófian descriptions—those that would rather omit ornament than pursue recognition of having been written with the "inspired" flow of a native speaker—the complacent reader is introduced to profound uncertainties. There is some part of readership that is complacency; we go in feeling that we have mastered letters—but the words of a rebel vocabulary don't feel chosen for their communicative properties so much as they feel repurposed to convey situations the speaker hasn't learned the "correct" words for. The reasons or excuses for not having learned the "correct" words are immaterial: ultimately those words haven't been learned, and here we are in the realm of Kristóf's best-known novel, *The Notebook,*[6] in which the twin protagonists study the connotations of human interactions such as giving, taking, helping and harming from scratch. This is where the sublime refinement of Ágota Kristóf's craft comes closest to knocking the breath out of our bodies: the pressure she brings to bear on words and what they do and do not say to us returns her readers to an awareness that the tangled, snapping network of systems that presents itself to us as "the world" is not legible and never has been. This reawakening might even place us somewhere close to the states we existed in before learning to read.

Do you remember much about your preliterate time?

My own memories of becoming a reader are mostly feelings of being engulfed by rage at having to deal with books, these boxes of signs with noises trapped inside them. (Just like TV, I suppose, but TV's advantage was that watching it demanded a much less keen attention.) Besides, how suspicious it all was, this reading business! Why was I required to know how to do it? So that I could learn other things, I was told. But why do we have to read and write words to know things? I don't think I ever actually asked anyone that question; I must have assumed it would answer itself once I'd crossed over to the other side of the comprehension barrier. I'm not sure, however, if I've found an answer. Text and the absorption of it is a key form of sustenance and of instruction as well as the means for the restoration of burned bridges between all manner of thoughts and ideas. And yet text and our absorption of it are the means by which language makes use of us for all manner of detrimental purposes—instilling a hatred of the other along with a love of categories and hierarchies that demean everyone even as they seem to elevate a worthy few. Or, in the caverns mere steps away from these loftier arenas, there's late night reading and rereading of text messages and email messages in attempts to pinpoint the exact source of insult, comfort or charm. Which combination of letters carries that? Suppose you couldn't read at all and the text or email were merely meaningless glyphs—wouldn't you just put yourself to bed then, or access overstimulation in other, far less neurotic ways?

These pros and cons of literacy will already have crossed your mind in terms more lucid than the ones I'm gesturing toward. *The Illiterate's* narrator exhibits signs of having weighed up the pros and cons of being text-susceptible to her own satisfaction, and exhibits no qualms when it comes to aligning herself with the unnatural act of interpreting text as a way of life. Having casually described her propensity to read as analogous to "a disease" in its seeming independence from her conscious desire, the irredeemable transgressor goes on to deliver a direct report of things people say when they catch her reading:

> *—She never does anything. She's always reading.*
> *—She doesn't know how to do anything else.*
> *—It's the most pointless activity that exists.*
> *—It's pure laziness.*

And above all:

> *—She reads instead of . . .*

—which is immediately followed by three words that encapsulate that most distinctively Kristóf air of part wry enquiry, part merciless challenge—

> *Instead of what?*

Such a train of thought leads to writing: some shame is felt for languishing in the (surface) passivity of reading instead of putting things into words. *The Illiterate* wonders if writing is the mightier act. In the last few lines of his 2014 poem "Onomatomania," Thomas Lux poses this question too (without the question mark, in terms that are just as much a goading of the unreal as they are an incitement for the unwritten to rise up):

> ... nothing is really real
> until it is written.
> Until it is written!
> Even those who cannot read
> know that.

Kristóf's "illiteracy" positions legibility as a battle of wills. After all, the written word can be so impatient with us when there's any sign of our not going along with the agreed-upon concepts that award it legitimacy. We hesitate a moment, and the reaction from the words we are unsure of generally goes along the lines of: Are you stupid?

I recently read that *Nowe Ateny*, the first Polish-language encyclopedia, had nothing but scorn for any eighteenth-century reader who expected a full debrief on the nature, deeds, and habits of horses. The entry begins:

> Horse: Everyone knows what a horse is.

Life's retort to this is that knowledge of the word and knowledge of the phenomenon referred to are different (albeit related) matters. Deeming a person who neither reads nor writes a know-nothing warps fact, and deeming a writer or a reader a know-it-all does the same thing. Can we enter into a relationship with language that holds a balance between verbal and nonverbal truths? Being a reader, and thereby wicked-minded, the temptation to experiment with recipes for reality proved too strong for the adolescent Kristóf to resist—in this book she recounts the "birth secret" prank she played on her little brother, luring the boy *into a corner of the garden* to tell him:

> *—So this is it—you're a foundling. You're not from a family. You were found in a field, abandoned and completely naked.*

We can't judge; it was words that made Kristóf do it, she had to test their power over her probably preliterate sibling by saying something that no text could either prove or disprove for him ...

There's at least one other kinship that helped this illiterate, *The Illiterate*, on her way. This book reveals Kristóf as an admirer and affirmer of the vitality of Thomas Bernhard's work, and I see that—I see their joint expansion of the vocabulary of rebellion. Kristof's Bernhard is the very same Bernhard whose monologue in the 1970 film *Drei Tage* states:

> *I am a story destroyer, I am the typical story destroyer.*
> *In my work, at the first sign of a story taking form, or if I catch sight of even a trace of a story, rising somewhere in the distance behind a mound of prose, I shoot it down.*
> *The same is true of sentences—I almost want to annihilate in advance whole sentences that even possibly could develop.*[7]

These are the acts of the well-informed illiterate. Well informed by experience, which shows that the written world is neither complete, nor does it complete any of the matters it touches upon. On top of all that, reading is a skill we're still acquiring. If the likes of Kristóf and her kin have anything to do with it, we shall never feel that we've finished learning to read. Our brushes with eternity lie in the scope of this schooling.

HELEN OYEYEMI

1. From Kristóf's 1999 interview with Riccardo Benedetti, translated from French by Will Heyward and published by *Music and Literature* in 2016: https://www.musicandliterature.org/features/2016/6/8/a-conversation-with-agota-kristof.

2. From Kristóf's 2011 interview with Dóra Szekeres: https://hlo.hu/interview/agota.html.

3. This isn't a claim that exile is inherently bitter, but that Kristóf's was tinged with fairly sharp regret. At the time of her 2006 interview with Gergely Negy, the author's evaluation of her departure from Hungary boils down to *I regret that I ever left*. And there's this in *The Illiterate*: *What would my life have been like if I hadn't left my country? More difficult, poorer, I think, but also less solitary, less torn. Happy, maybe.*

4. "*I worked in a factory where we weren't allowed to speak to each other much,*" interview with Benedetti.

5. *I have spoken in French for more than thirty years, I have written in French for twenty years, but I still don't know it. I don't speak it without mistakes, and I can only write it with the help of dictionaries, which I frequently consult.*

6. Published in 1986, with Alan Sheridan's English translation published in 1988.

7. Thomas Bernhard, *Three Days, from the Film by Ferry Radax*, trans. and ed. Laura Lindgren (New York: Blast Books, 2016), 89.

THE ILLITERATE

Beginnings

I read. It is like a disease. I read everything that comes to hand, everything that meets my glance: newspapers, schoolbooks, posters, bits of paper found on the street, recipes, children's books. Everything in print.

I am four years old. The war has just begun.

At this time we are living in a small village that has no railroad station, no electricity, no running water, and no telephone.

My father is the only schoolteacher in the village. He teaches all the grades, from the first to the sixth, in the same classroom. The school is separated from our house by only the schoolyard, and its windows look out onto my mother's vegetable garden. When I climb up to the last window of the schoolroom, I see the whole class with my father standing at the front, writing on the blackboard.

My father's classroom smells of chalk, ink, paper, calm, silence and snow, even in summer.

My mother's large kitchen smells of slaughtered animals, boiled meat, milk, jam, bread, wet laundry, baby's pee, agitation, noise, and summer heat, even in winter.

When the weather is too poor for us to play out of doors, when the baby screams louder than usual, when my brother and I make too much noise and kick up too much of a ruckus in the kitchen, our mother sends us to our father for a "punishment."

We go outside. My brother stops by the shed where the firewood is stored.

—I'd rather stay here. I'll chop up some kindling.

—Yes. Mother will be pleased.

I cross the courtyard, enter the classroom. I stop near the door, lower my eyes. My father says:

—Come closer.

I come closer. I speak into his ear.

—Punished . . . My mother . . .

—Is that all?

He asks "Is that all?" because sometimes there is a note from my mother that I must hand over without saying anything, or a word I have to pronounce: "doctor," "emergency," or sometimes just a number: 38 or 40. All because of the baby who is always catching childhood diseases.

I say to my father:

—No. That's all.

He hands me a picture book.

—Go sit down.

I go to the back of the classroom where there are always extra places behind the oldest pupils.

It is thus that, at a very young age, without taking any notice of it and completely by chance, I catch the incurable disease of reading.

When we visit my mother's parents who live in a nearby city, in a house with electricity and running water, my grandfather takes me by the hand and we make the rounds of the neighborhood together.

Grandfather takes a newspaper from the big pocket of his greatcoat and says to the neighbors:

—Look! Listen!

And to me:

—Read.

And I read. Fluently, without mistakes, as quickly as I am asked.

Apart from this grandfatherly pride, my reading disease brings me mostly reproaches and scorn.

—She never does anything. She's always reading.

—She doesn't know how to do anything else.

—It's the most pointless activity that exists.

—It's pure laziness.

And above all:

—She reads instead of ...

Instead of what?

—There are far more useful things to do, no?

Even now, in the morning, when the house grows empty and all my neighbors leave for work, I feel a little bit guilty when I sit down at the kitchen table to read the newspapers for hours, instead of ... doing the housework, or washing last night's dishes, or going out to do the shopping, or washing and ironing the laundry, or making jam or cakes ...

And above all, above all! Instead of writing.

From speech to writing

Even as a small child, I like to tell stories. Stories invented by myself.

Sometimes Grandmother comes to visit from the city, to help Mother. In the evening, it is she who puts us to bed. She tries to lull us to sleep with tales we have already heard a hundred times.

I get out of bed and tell Grandmother:

—I'm the one who's going to tell the stories, not you.

She takes me on her knees, rocks me.

—You tell, you tell then.

I begin with a sentence, any sentence, and the rest follows. Characters appear, die, or disappear. There are good characters and evil ones, poor and rich, winners and losers. There is no end to the story I stammer on Grandmother's knees.

—And then . . . and then . . .

Grandmother settles me into my cot, lowers the wick of the petrol lamp and goes out into the kitchen.

My brothers are asleep, I too fall asleep, and in my dream the story continues, beautiful and terrifying.

What I like best is to tell stories to my little brother Tila. He is our mother's favorite. He is three years younger than

I am, so he believes everything I say. For example, I lure him into a corner of the garden and ask:

—Do you want me to tell you a secret?

—What secret?

—The secret of your birth.

—There's no secret about my birth.

—Yes, there is. But I'll tell you only if you swear not to tell anybody.

—I swear.

—So this is it—you're a foundling. You're not from our family. You were found in a field, abandoned, completely naked.

Tila says:

—It's not true.

—My parents are going to tell you later, when you're older. If you knew how pitiful you looked, all skinny and naked . . .

Tila starts to cry. I take him in my arms.

—Don't cry. I love you as much as if you were my real brother.

—As much as Yano?

—Almost as much. Yano's my real brother, after all.

Tila thinks for a minute.

—So how come I have the same last name as you? And how come Mother loves me more than you two? You and Yano are always being punished. I'm never punished.

I explain.

—You have the same last name, because you were officially adopted. And Mother is nicer to you than to us because she wants to show that she doesn't make any distinction between you and her real children.

—I am her real child!

Tila screams, he runs towards the house.

—Mama! Mama!

I run after him.

—You swore not to tell. I was just kidding.

Too late. Tila arrives in the kitchen and throws himself into Mother's arms.

—Tell me I'm your son. Your real son. You're my real mother.

I am punished, of course, for telling tales. I kneel down on a corn cob in a corner of the bedroom. Soon Yano arrives with another corn cob and kneels down next to me.

I ask him:

—Why are you being punished?

—I don't know. I just patted Tila on the head and said "I love you, little bastard."

We laugh. I know he tried to get punished on purpose, out of solidarity, and also because he is bored without me.

I tell Tila many other tales, I also try with Yano, but he doesn't believe me because he is one year older than I am.

The desire to write comes later, when the silver thread of childhood is severed, when the bad times arrive, the years when I will say "I don't like them."

When, separated from my parents and my brothers, I leave for boarding school in an unknown city and, in order to bear the pain of separation, only one solution will remain: to write.

Poems

When I arrive at boarding school, I am fourteen. Yano, my brother, has already been in boarding school for a year, but in a different city. Tila is still at home with Mother.

This is not a boarding school for girls from wealthy families; it is more the opposite. It is somewhere between a barracks and a convent, between an orphanage and a reform school.

There are around two hundred girls aged fourteen to eighteen, all given free bed and board by the State.

We live in dormitory rooms that house from ten to twenty girls, with bunk beds lined with straw mattresses and grey blankets. Our narrow metal cupboards are in the corridor.

A bell wakes us at six in the morning and a sleepy monitor checks all the rooms. Some of the pupils hide under their beds; others run down to the courtyard. After three rounds in the courtyard, we do exercises for ten minutes; then, still running, we go back upstairs. We wash with cold water, put on our clothes, go down to the refectory. Our breakfast consists of coffee with milk and a slice of bread.

Yesterday's mail is handed out—letters already opened by the administration. Their justification is:

—You are minors. We are replacing your parents.

At seven thirty, we leave for school in serried ranks, singing revolutionary songs as we cross the city. Boys stop as we go by. They whistle, yelling compliments or coarse words.

When we return from school, we eat our midday meal, then head to our study halls where we stay until supper.

In the study halls, complete silence is required.

What can we do during these long hours? Our homework, of course, but that, as it is utterly uninteresting, is quickly done. We are also allowed to read, but we have only "compulsory" books that are quickly read, and these books, for the most part, are also completely lacking in interest.

So during these long hours of enforced silence, I start writing a kind of journal. I even invent a secret handwriting so that nobody can read what I have written. I note down my troubles, my sorrows, my sadness, everything that makes me cry silently at night in my bed.

I cry over the loss of my brothers, of my parents, of our family home now inhabited by strangers.

Above all I cry over my lost freedom.

It is true we are free to receive visits on Sunday afternoons in the "sitting room," even visits from boys, in the presence of a monitor. We are also free to walk in town, even with boys, on Sunday afternoons, but only on the main street. A monitor walks there too.

But I am not free to go and see my brother Yano who is only twenty kilometers away, who is in the same situation as I am, and who cannot come and visit me either. We are not allowed to leave the city, and anyway we don't have the money for the train fare.

I also cry over my childhood, our childhood as a threesome, Yano, Tila and me.

No more racing barefoot through the forest on the damp earth until we reach "the blue rock'; no more trees to climb or fall down from when a rotten branch gives way; no more Yano to pick me up when I fall; no more nighttime strolls on the roofs; no more Tila to tattle on us to Mother.

At boarding school, lights out is at 10 p.m. A monitor patrols all the rooms.

I continue to read, if I have a book, by the light of the street lamp. Then, as I cry myself to sleep, phrases are born out of the night. They circle around me, whispering, taking on rhythm and rhymes, they sing, they become poems.

Before, everything was more beautiful,
The music in the trees
The wind in my hair
And in your outstretched hands
The Sun.

Clowning

The 1950s. Aside from a handful of privileged individuals, everyone in our country is poor. Some are even poorer than others.

At boarding school, to be sure, we are provided for. We are fed, and we have a roof over our heads, but the food is so dreadful and in such insufficient quantity that we are always hungry. In winter we are cold. At school we keep our coats on and we stand up every fifteen minutes to do gymnastic exercises to warm ourselves up. In our dormitories it is just as cold. We sleep with our socks on, and when we go upstairs to our study halls, we have to take our blankets with us.

At this time, I wear Yano's old coat that is too small for him — a black coat without buttons, torn on the left side.

A boy will tell me years later:

— How I admired you with your black coat that was always open, even in winter.

On my way to school, I carry a girlfriend's schoolbag because I don't have one of my own, and I have to put my notebooks and schoolbooks in hers. The schoolbag is heavy and my fingers freeze because I don't have any gloves. I don't have a pencil or a pen either, or gym clothes. I borrow everything.

I also borrow a pair of shoes when I have to take mine to the shoemaker to be repaired.

If I have to give them back, I stay in bed for three days because of the shoemaker. I can't tell the directress of the boarding school that I don't have an extra pair of shoes to go to school in. I tell her I am sick and she believes me because I am a good student. She touches my forehead and says:

—You have a fever. At least 38. Cover up well.

I cover up well. But how am I going to pay the shoemaker? It is out of the question to ask my parents for money. Father is in prison and we have had no news of him for years. Mother works wherever she can. She lives in a single room with Tila, and the neighbors sometimes let them use their kitchen.

For a short time, Mother works in the city where I am studying. Once, on my way home from school, I go to visit her. The place is a small basement room where a dozen women seated around a large table are packaging rat poison by the light of a single light bulb.

My mother asks:

—Is everything all right?

I say:

—Yes, everything is fine. Don't worry.

She doesn't ask me if I need anything. I say anyway:

—I don't need anything. How is Tila?

My mother says:

—He's fine. He'll be going to boarding school too, in the fall.

We have nothing else to say to each other. I would like to say that I have had my shoes repaired, that the shoe-maker has given me credit and that I have to pay him back as soon as possible, but when I look at my mother's ragged dress, her gloves soiled by rat poison, I can't say any of that. I kiss Mother goodbye. I leave and don't come back again.

To earn a little money, I organize performances at school during the twenty-minute recess. I write sketches that, with two or three girlfriends, we learn overnight, sometimes inventing new ones on the spot. My specialty is imitating the teachers. In the morning, we spread the news to some of the classes, the next day to others. The entrance fee is the same as the price of the crescent rolls that the concierge sells during recess.

Our performances are a great success; the spectators spill out into the corridor. Even some of the teachers come, forcing me to make last-minute changes in the subjects of my imitations.

I carry the experience over to the dormitories, with different girlfriends and different sketches. In the evening, we go from room to room. The girls beg us to come; they prepare veritable feasts for us from the parcels the farm girls receive from their parents. We, the actresses, accept either money or food, but our greatest reward is the joy of making others laugh.

Mother tongue and enemy languages

In the beginning, there was only one language. Objects, things, feelings, colors, dreams, letters, books, newspapers were this language.

I couldn't imagine that another language could exist, that a human being could pronounce a word that I wouldn't be able to understand.

In my mother's kitchen, in my father's school, in Uncle Geza's church, in the streets, in the village houses and also in my grandparents' city, everyone spoke the same language, and there was never any question of another.

It was said that the gypsies, who lived on the outskirts of the village, spoke another language, but I thought it wasn't a true language, it was only a language they spoke amongst themselves, like my brother Yano and I when we spoke in such a way that our little brother Tila wouldn't be able to understand.

I also thought that the gypsies did this because in the village café they had specially marked glasses, glasses just for them, because nobody wanted to drink from a glass that a gypsy had drunk from.

It was also said that the gypsies stole children. It is true they stole a great many things, but when we walked past their homes built of clay and saw the numbers of children playing out in front of these hovels, we wondered why they would want to steal others. And when the gypsies came into the village to sell their pottery or their baskets woven from reeds, they spoke "normally," the same language as we did.

When I was nine years old, we moved. We went to live in a city on the border where at least a quarter of the population spoke German. For us, the Hungarians, this was an enemy language, because it was a reminder of Austrian domination, and it was also the language of the foreign soldiers who were occupying our country at this time.

One year later, our country was occupied by other foreign soldiers. The Russian language became obligatory at school and all other foreign languages were forbidden.

Nobody speaks Russian. The teachers who teach foreign languages—German, French, English—take accelerated Russian classes for a few months, but they don't really know the language and have no desire to teach it. And anyway, the pupils have no desire to learn it.

What we witness here is a national and intellectual sabotage, a natural and passive resistance, unplanned and requiring no explanation.

The same lack of enthusiasm accompanies the teaching and learning of the geography, history and literature of the Soviet Union. A generation of dunces graduates from high school.

It is in this way that, at the age of twenty-one, when I arrive in Switzerland and when, completely by chance, I arrive in a city where French is spoken, I confront a language that is totally unknown to me. It is here that my battle to conquer this language begins, a long and arduous battle that will last my entire life.

I have spoken French for more than thirty years, I have written in French for twenty years, but I still don't know it. I don't speak it without mistakes, and I can only write it with the help of dictionaries, which I frequently consult.

It is for this reason that I also call the French language an enemy language. There is a further reason, the most serious of all: this language is killing my mother tongue.

Stalin's death

March 1953. Stalin is dead. We learned the news last night. Sorrow is obligatory at the boarding school. We go to bed without speaking. In the morning we ask:

—Is it a holiday?

The monitor says:

—No. You'll go to school as usual. But no singing.

We go to school as usual, in ranks, but without singing. Red flags and black flags flutter on buildings.

Our teacher is waiting for us. He says:

—At eleven o'clock, the school bell will ring. You will stand up to observe a minute of silence. In the meantime, you will write a composition on the following subject: "The Death of Stalin." In this composition, you will write down everything Comrade Stalin meant to you. A father first of all, then a beacon of light.

One of the girls bursts into tears. The teacher says:

—Take hold of yourself, Miss. We are all sad beyond measure. But let us try to conquer our pain. Your compositions will not be graded, considering that you are all in a state of shock.

We write. The teacher walks up and down the classroom, his hands behind his back.

A bell rings. We stand up. The teacher looks at his watch. The sirens of the city should also sound. A girl standing by the window looks out into the street and says:

—It's only the bell for the garbage pails.

We sit down again, giggling uncontrollably.

Soon afterwards the school bell rings and the city sirens sound. We stand up again, but because of the garbage pails, we are still laughing. We stand for one long minute, shaking with silent laughter, and our teacher laughs with us.

I carried the color photograph of Stalin in my pocket for many years, but at his death I understood why my aunt had torn it up during one of my visits.

The indoctrination was vast, and it was particularly effective on young minds. Rudolf Nureyev, the great dissident Russian dancer, describes it thus: "The day Stalin died, I went outside, into the countryside. I waited for something extraordinary to happen, for nature to respond to the tragedy. Nothing happened. No earthquake, no sign."

No. The "earthquake" did not occur until thirty-six years later, and it wasn't a reply from nature, but from the people. It had taken all those years for the "Father" of us all to truly die, for our "beacon of light" to be extinguished—forever, let us hope.

How many victims did he have on his conscience? Nobody knows. In Romania, the deaths are still being counted; in Hungary, there were thirty thousand in 1956. What we will never be able to measure is the pernicious role the dictatorship exerted on the philosophy, art and literature of the countries of Eastern Europe. By imposing its ideology on these countries, the Soviet Union not only obstructed their economic development, it also tried to stifle their national culture and identity.

To my knowledge, no Russian dissident writer has ever addressed or mentioned this issue. What do they think, those who suffered under their tyrant, what do they think about those "unimportant little countries" that suffered in addition under foreign domination, *their* domination? That of *their* country. Are they ashamed of it, or will they be ashamed one day?

Here, I think of Thomas Bernhard, the great Austrian writer, who never ceased to criticize and to denounce his country, his era, and the society in which he lived—with hate and with love, and also with humor.

He died on 12 February 1989. For him, there was no national or international day of mourning, no false tears, and perhaps no real tears either. Only his devoted readers, among whom I count myself, realized what an immense loss for literature it was; Thomas Bernhard would no longer write. Worse still: he had prohibited his unpublished manuscripts from ever being published.

That was the last "no" to society from the brilliant author of the book entitled *Yes*. This book is here on the table in front of me, along with *Concrete*, *The Loser*, *The Voice Imitator*, *Woodcutters* and others. *Yes* is the first book of his that I read. I lent it to several friends, telling them that I had never laughed so hard when reading a book. They returned it without being able to read it to the end, so "demoralizing" and "unbearable" did they find it. As for its "comic" side, they had truly not seen it anywhere.

It is true that the content is terrible, for this "yes" is indeed a "yes," but a "yes" to death, and thus "no" to life.

Nevertheless, whether or not he wishes it to be so, Thomas Bernhard will live on eternally as an example to all those who claim to be writers.

Memory

I learn from the newspapers and the television that a ten-year-old Turkish child has died of exhaustion and exposure while illegally crossing the Swiss border with his parents. The "smugglers" left them near the border. They had only to walk straight ahead until they reached the first Swiss village. They walked for hours through the mountains and the forest. It was very cold. Toward the end, the father carried the child on his back. But it was already too late. When they reached the village, the child was dead of fatigue, exposure and exhaustion.

My first reaction is that of any Swiss citizen: "How could people have embarked on such a risky adventure with children? Such irresponsibility is unacceptable." The shock I receive in return is violent and immediate. A cold, end-of-November wind sweeps through my well-heated room, and the voice of memory rises up inside me with stupefaction: "What? Have you completely forgotten? You did the same thing, exactly the same thing. And your own child was practically a newborn."

Yes, I remember.

I am twenty-one. I have been married for two years, and I have a little daughter who is four months old. We are crossing the border between Hungary and Austria on an evening in November, led by a smuggler. His name is Joseph and I know him well.

We are a group of about ten people, including several children. My little daughter is asleep in her father's arms, and I am carrying two bags. One holds baby bottles, diapers, and clean clothes for the baby; the other holds dictionaries. We walk in silence behind Joseph for about an hour. It is almost completely dark. Now and then electric flares and floodlights illuminate everything. We hear the crackling and shots of rifles; then silence and darkness take over again.

At the edge of the forest Joseph stops and says to us:

—You are in Austria. All you have to do is walk straight ahead. The village is not far.

I embrace Joseph. All of us give him the money we have; in any case, this money will be of no value in Austria.

We walk through the forest. For a long time. Too long. Branches tear at our faces, we fall into holes, dead leaves wet our shoes, we twist our ankles on tree roots. A few flashlights have been switched on, but they only illuminate little circles of light, and trees—always more trees. Yet we should already have come out of the forest. We have the feeling that we are walking in circles.

A child says:

—I'm afraid. I want to go home. I want to go to sleep.

Another child cries. A woman says:

—We're lost.

A young man says:

—Everyone, stop. If we continue like this, we'll wind

up back in Hungary, if it's not already too late. Stay where you are. I'll go see.

We all know what winding up back in Hungary means: prison for having illegally crossed the border, and maybe even being shot by drunken Russian border guards.

The young man climbs up a tree. When he comes down, he says:

—I know where we are. I've used the lights to get my bearings. Follow me.

We follow him. Soon, the forest thins out and finally we are walking on a real path, without branches, without holes, without tree roots.

Suddenly a powerful lamp lights us up. A voice says:

—Halt!

One of us says in German:

—We are refugees.

The Austrian border guards reply, laughing:

—That's what we thought. Come with us.

They lead us to the village square. A whole crowd of refugees is there. The mayor arrives.

—Those with children, step forward.

We are put up with a family of farmers. They are very kind. They take care of the baby, they give us food to eat, they give us a bed.

What is strange is the dearth of memories I have kept of all of this. It is as if everything took place in a dream, or in a different life. As if my memory refused to remember this moment when I lost a large part of my life.

In Hungary I left my journal with its secret handwriting, and also my first poems. I left my brothers, my parents, without any warning, without saying farewell or goodbye. But above all, that day, that day at the end of November 1956, I lost forever my sense of belonging to a people.

Displaced persons

From the little Austrian village where we arrived from Hungary, we take the coach for Vienna. The mayor of the village pays for our tickets. During the voyage my little daughter sleeps on my lap. All along the road, luminous mileposts flash by. I have never seen such mileposts before.

When we arrive in Vienna, we go to a police station to announce our presence. There, in the office, I change my baby's diapers and give her her bottle. She throws up. The policemen give us the address of a refugee center and tell us which tramway will take us there for free. In the tram, well-dressed women take my baby on their laps, they slip money into my pocket.

The center is a large building that must have been a factory or a barracks. In immense rooms, straw mattresses are spread out on the floor. There are collective showers and a vast dining hall. At the entrance to the dining hall is a blackboard stuck with notices of missing persons. People are looking for relatives and friends they lost contact with during the border crossing, beforehand or afterwards, in the city of Vienna, or even in the crowd and the chaos of the center.

My husband, like everyone else, spends his days waiting in the offices of different embassies in order to find a host country. I stay with my little daughter who lies on the straw mattress and babbles as she plays with bits of straw. I am obliged to learn a few words of German to ask for what I need for the baby. Taking her in my arms, I enter the center's big kitchen and say to the man who seems to be the manager: "Milch für Kinder, bitte." Or "Seife für Kinder." The man always gives me personally what I ask for.

Christmas is coming when we take the train to Switzerland. There are fir branches decorating the little shelf in front of the window, and chocolate and oranges. This is a special train. Aside from the people accompanying us, the only travellers are Hungarians, and the train makes no stops until the Swiss border. There, a fanfare welcomes us, and kind women hand goblets of hot tea through the window, and chocolate and oranges.

We arrive in Lausanne. We are lodged in a barracks high above the city, next to a soccer field. Young women dressed like soldiers take our children with reassuring smiles. Men and women are separated for the showers. Our clothes are taken away to be disinfected.

Those among us who have already lived through a similar experience confess later on that they have been very frightened. We are all relieved to find each other again afterwards and, above all, to find our children, clean and already well fed. My little girl is sleeping peacefully in a beautiful crib the likes of which she has never had before, next to my bed.

On Sunday, after the soccer game, the spectators come to look at us through the barracks fence. They offer us chocolate and oranges, naturally, but also cigarettes and even money. It no longer reminds us of concentration camps, but of a zoo. The more modest among us refrain from going out into the courtyard, while others spend their time reaching their hands through the fence and comparing their bounty.

Several times a week, factory owners come looking for workers. Friends and acquaintances find a job and a flat. They depart, leaving their addresses.

After a month in Lausanne, we spend another month in Zurich, lodged in a school in a forest. We are given language lessons, but I can attend only rarely, because of my little girl.

What would my life have been like if I hadn't left my country? More difficult, poorer, I think, but also less solitary, less torn. Happy, maybe.

What I am certain of is that I would have written, no matter where I was, in no matter what language.

The desert

From the refugee center in Zurich, we are "distributed" to places all around Switzerland. This is how, by chance, we come to Neuchâtel, more precisely to Valangin, where a two-room apartment, furnished by the inhabitants of the village, awaits us. A few weeks later, I begin work at a clock factory in Fontainemelon.

I get up at five thirty. I feed and dress my baby, I get dressed too, and I catch the six-thirty bus that will take me to the factory. I leave my child at the crèche and go inside the factory. I come out again at five in the evening. I pick up my little girl at the crèche, I take the bus again, I go back home. I do the shopping at the village shop, make the fire (the apartment does not have central heating), prepare the evening meal, put the child to bed, do the washing-up, write a little, and I too go to bed.

The factory is a good place for writing poems. The work is monotonous, you can think about other things, and the machines have a regular rhythm that accentuates the lines of verse. In my drawer I keep a sheet of paper and a pencil. When the poem takes shape, I note it down. In the evening, I copy it out in a notebook.

We are about ten Hungarians who work in the factory.

We sit together during the lunch break at the canteen, but the food is so different from what we are used to that we eat almost nothing. In my own case, for at least a year, I have only coffee with milk and some bread for the midday meal.

At the factory, everyone is kind to us. They smile at us, they speak to us, but we don't understand.

It is here that the desert begins. A social desert, a cultural desert. After the exaltation of the days of revolution and escape, come silence, emptiness, nostalgia for the days when we felt we were participating in something important, even historic, homesickness, and the lack of family and friends.

We were waiting for something when we arrived here. We didn't know what we were waiting for, but it was certainly not this: these days of dismal work, these silent evenings, this frozen life, without change, without surprise, without hope.

Materially speaking, we are a little better off than before. We have two rooms instead of one. We have enough coal and sufficient amounts of food. But compared to what we have lost, we are paying too high a price.

On the bus in the morning, the ticket-taker sits down next to me. In the morning it is always the same one, fat and jovial. He talks to me for the whole ride. I don't understand him very well; I understand nevertheless that he wants to reassure me by explaining that the Swiss will never allow the Russians to enter the country. He says that I must not be afraid any longer, that I must no longer be sad, that now I am safe. I smile. I can't tell him that I'm not afraid of the Russians, and that if I'm sad, it's more because

I'm too safe at present, and because there is nothing else to do or to think about than the job, the factory, the shopping, the laundry, the meals, and nothing else to wait for but Sundays when I can sleep and dream a little longer about my country.

How can I explain to him, without hurting his feelings, and with the few French words I know, that his beautiful country is a desert for us, the refugees, a desert we must cross in order to arrive at what is called "integration," "assimilation." At that time, I don't yet know that some of us will never arrive.

Two of our number returned to Hungary despite the prison sentence that awaited them. Two others, young bachelors, went farther, to the United States, to Canada. Four others went even farther, as far as one can go, beyond the great boundary. These four people of my acquaintance killed themselves during the first two years of our exile. One with barbiturates, one with gas, and two others with the rope. The youngest was eighteen. Her name was Gisèle.

How do you become a writer?

First of all, naturally, you must write. Then, you must continue to write. Even when it doesn't interest anyone. Even when you feel that it will never interest anyone. Even when the manuscripts pile up in the drawers and you forget them, while writing new ones.

When I arrived in Switzerland, my hopes of becoming a writer were just about nil. It is true that I published a few poems in a Hungarian literary review, but my chances, my possibilities of being published ended there. And when, after long years of hard work, I was able to finish two plays written in French, I didn't really know what to do with them, where to send them, or to whom.

My first performed play, entitled *John and Joe*, was presented in a bistro, at the Café du Marché in Neuchâtel. On Fridays and Saturdays, after the evening meal, a few amateur actors organized "evening cabarets" there. Thus began my "career" as a playwright. The success of this play, which was performed for several months, brought me great happiness at the time and encouraged me to continue writing.

Two years later, another of my plays was produced at

the Théâtre de la Tarentule, in Saint-Aubin, a small village near Neuchâtel. This time too it was performed by amateur actors.

My "career" seems as though it will end there, and my dozens of manuscripts slowly turn yellow on a bookshelf. Fortunately, someone advises me to send my texts to the radio, and it is the beginning of another "career," that of a radio dramatist. Here, my texts are now performed, or rather read, by professional actors, and I receive real royalties. Between 1978 and 1983, Radio Suisse Romande* produces five of my plays; I am even commissioned to write a play for the Year of the Child.

I haven't, however, abandoned the theatre. In 1983, I agree to work with the theatre school of the Neuchâtel cultural center. My work consists in writing a play specifically intended for fifteen students. This work pleases me very much. I attend all the rehearsals.

The classes generally begin with all kinds of physical exercises. These exercises remind me of the ones we did when we were children, my brother and I, or a girlfriend and I. Exercises devoted to silence, to immobility, to fasting . . . I begin to write short texts based on my childhood memories. I am still far from imagining that these short texts will one day become a book. And yet, two years later, on my desk is a large notebook that contains a coherent story, with a beginning and an end, like a real novel. I still have to type it, correct it, type it again, eliminate everything there is too much of, correct it over and over, until I think the text is presentable. Here again, I don't really

---

* Translator's note: the Swiss French-language radio station.

know what to do with the manuscript. Who should it be sent to, given to? I don't know a single editor, and I don't know anyone who does. I think vaguely about sending it to L'Âge d'Homme, but a friend tells me, "You have to start with the big three in Paris." He brings me the addresses of the three publishing houses: Gallimard, Grasset, Seuil. I make three copies of the manuscript, I prepare three packages, I write three identical letters: "Dear Sir ..."

On the day I mail it all out, I announce to my older daughter:

—I've finished my novel.

She says:

—Really? And do you think someone will publish it?

I say:

—Yes, certainly.

Indeed, I do not doubt it for a minute. I have the conviction, the certitude that my novel is a good novel, and that it will be published without any difficulty. Thus I am more surprised than disappointed when, after four or five weeks, my manuscript comes back from Gallimard and then from Grasset, accompanied by a polite and impersonal rejection letter. I tell myself that I must look for the addresses of other publishers when, one afternoon in November, I receive a phone call. The caller is Gilles Carpentier of Éditions du Seuil. He tells me that he has just read my manuscript, and that it has been years since he has read anything so beautiful. He tells me that he reread it completely after reading it a first time, and that he thinks he will publish it. But first he needs to obtain the consent of several people. He will call back in a few weeks. He calls back one week later, saying, "I'm writing up your contract."

Three years later, I walk through the streets of Berlin with my translator, Erika Tophoven. We stop in front of bookstores. In their display windows is my second novel. At home, in my house, on a shelf, is *The Notebook*, translated into eighteen languages.

In Berlin, in the evening, we participate in a reading. People come to see me, to hear me, to ask me questions. About my books, about my life, about my itinerary as a writer. Here is the answer to the question: you become a writer by writing with patience and obstinacy, without ever losing faith in what you write.

The illiterate

One day, my neighbor and friend says to me:

—I saw a television programme about foreign women workers. They work all day in a factory, and they do the housework and take care of their children in the evening.

I say:

—That's what I did when I arrived in Switzerland.

She says:

—And they don't even know French.

—I didn't know it either.

My friend is upset. She can't tell me the amazing story about foreign women that she saw on television. She has forgotten my past so well that she can't imagine that I once belonged to this race of women who don't know the language of the country, who work in factories and who take care of their families in the evening.

But I remember. The factory, the grocery shopping, the child, the meals. And the unknown language. At the factory, it is difficult to speak together. The machines make too much noise. We can talk only in the toilets, while we quickly smoke a cigarette.

My female coworkers teach me the basics. They say, "The weather is nice," showing me the landscape of the

Val-de-Ruz. They touch me to teach me other words: hair, arm, hands, mouth, nose.

In the evening, I come home with the child. My little daughter looks at me wide-eyed when I speak to her in Hungarian.

One time, she begins to cry because I don't understand her; another time, because she doesn't understand me.

Five years after arriving in Switzerland, I speak French, but I can't read it. I have become illiterate once again. I, who knew how to read at the age of four.

I know words. When I read them, I don't recognize them. The letters correspond to nothing. Hungarian is a phonetic language. French is the exact opposite.

I don't know how I managed to live for five years without reading. There was, once a month, the *Hungarian Literary Gazette*, which published my poems at that time; there were also Hungarian books, mostly books that we had already read, which we received by post from the Geneva library, but no matter, it is better to reread than not to read at all. And fortunately, there was my writing.

My child will soon be six years old, she will start school.

I too start school, I start over. At the age of twenty-six, I enrol in summer school at the University of Neuchâtel, in order to learn how to read. These are classes intended for foreign students. There are British students, Americans, Germans, Japanese, Swiss-Germans. The entrance test is a written exam. I am hopeless. I am put in the class with the beginners.

After a few lessons, the teacher says to me:

—You speak French very well. What are you doing in the beginners' class?

I tell him:

—I don't know how to read or write. I'm illiterate.

He laughs.

—We'll see about that.

Two years later, I obtain my Certificate of French Studies, with honors.

I can read. I know how to read again. I can read Victor Hugo, Rousseau, Voltaire, Sartre, Camus, Michaux, Francis Ponge, Sade—everything I want to read in French—and also non-French authors, in translation, Faulkner, Steinbeck, Hemingway. The world is full of books—books that are understandable, at last, by me too.

I will have two more children. With them, I will practice reading, spelling, conjugation.

When they ask me what a certain word means, or how to spell it, I will never say:

—I don't know.

I will say:

—I'll go and look.

And I go and look in the dictionary; tirelessly, I go and look. I develop a passion for the dictionary.

I know I will never write French as native French writers do, but I will write it as I am able to, as best I can.

I did not choose this language. It was imposed on me by fate, by chance, by circumstance.

Writing in French is something I am obliged to do. It is a challenge.

The challenge of an illiterate.

ON ÁGOTA KRISTÓF

Every now and again you read a book by an unknown author and you know immediately that you are in the company of greatness. That is a rare and precious feeling. It happened to me when, a few years ago, a friend sent me a copy of Ágota Kristóf's first novel, *Le Grand Cahier* (*The Notebook*). The utter simplicity of the style, the clarity, the unflinching gaze at a world far removed from any I had experienced and yet curiously familiar—that of a peasant culture on the border of what we take to be Hungary and Germany in the dying moments of World War II—and the deep humanity underlying it all, took my breath away.

L'analphabète (here translated as *The Illiterate*), the short memoir she published in 2004, eighteen years after that dazzling debut, explains how it came about. Ágota Kristóf was born in a Hungarian village in 1935. Her father was the local schoolmaster, all the children in the school clustering together in the one classroom. In 1949, at fourteen, her father was imprisoned, we must presume for falling foul of the Communist authorities, and she was separated from her adored older brother and sent to boarding school, where in her distress she began to write. In November 1956, in the wake of the Russian crackdown on the Hungarian uprising, now married and with a child, she and her family crossed the border on foot with a group of other refugees and sought refuge first in Austria and

then in Switzerland. They eventually settled in Neuchâtel, where she found work in a factory. Once again her
sorrow—at being cut off from her parents and siblings,
her language and her native land—was the spur to writing. But in what language to write? The Hungarian she
was inward with but knew she would never be able to use
naturally again, or the French she heard all around her but
which lacked, for her, what she felt to be essential to a
living language? Laboriously, like a child, she set out to
master the language of the country in which she would
probably spend the rest of her life. Eventually she felt con-
fident enough to write it, and she even put on a few plays
in the factory to bring some amusement to the lives of
herself and her fellow workers.

She also began jotting down lightly fictionalized memories of growing up with her brother in their Hungarian
village. Each memory consisted of a bare couple of pages.
But soon they had taken on a life of their own and she
found herself with an entire novel, the story of twin boys,
sent by their mother to live with their grandmother in a
village on the Hungarian border to avoid the bombing (at
least that is the inference; there are no names of countries or cities in this book, nor any reference to historical
events). The grandmother, known locally as "The Witch"
and rumored to have poisoned her husband years before,
lives in utter poverty and unimaginable squalor, hoarding
under her bed what money she makes by renting a room
to an officer from the town and selling the few extra vegetables she grows. She makes her grandchildren work for
their food, sells the clothes their mother has given her for
them and purloins the money she regularly sends them.

The boys react to their new situation in an extraordinary way. Instead of retreating into sullenness and self-pity they make the decision to present a facade of imperturbable strength to the world, doing more in the garden and with the vegetables than their grandmother has asked of them, teaching themselves to read and write, hardening their bodies by whipping each other with their belts, lying in silence for hours, gradually finding ways to lead a decent and almost normal life in the midst of the filth and degradation of the grandmother's pigsty of a house.

To learn to write they undertake to describe what is happening to them, always referring to themselves in the first person plural:

> We start to write. We have two hours to write about the subject and two sheets of paper at our disposal.
>
> At the end of two hours we exchange our sheets of paper, each of us corrects the other's spelling mistakes with the help of the dictionary and, at the bottom of the page, writes: "Good" or "Not good." If it's "Not good," we throw the composition in the fire and try to write about the same subject in the next lesson. If it's "Good," we can copy out the composition into the Big Notebook.
>
> To decide whether it is "Good" or "Not good," we have a very simple rule: the composition must be true. We must describe what is, what we see, what we hear, what we do.
>
> For example, it is forbidden to write: "Grandmother is like a witch," but we are allowed to write: "People call Grandmother the Witch."
>
> It is forbidden to write: "The Little Town is beautiful," because the Little Town may be beautiful for us and ugly for someone else.

> *Similarly, if we write: "The batman is nice," this isn't
> a truth, because the batman may be capable of nasty acts
> that we know nothing about. So we would simply write:
> "The batman has given us some blankets."*

This, in effect, is Agota Kristof's own credo, and explains why her books are, thankfully, free of the overwriting which one finds in so much of the best postwar Hungarian authors, such as Kertész and Krasznahorkai.

The ending of the book is as shocking as anything in literature, all the more so for the quiet way it is narrated. But the shocks have been there all the way through, in the cold description of the hare-lipped neighbor's daughter, desperate for someone to love her, offering to suck their cocks and then caught inciting the dog to mount her; in the punishment they mete out to the charming and lively maid of the local priest, who has bathed them and washed their hair and is always ready to do them favors, but who they then see taunting and baiting a bedraggled line of Jewish prisoners passing through the village on their way to the railway station. Ágota Kristóf, through her clear-eyed twins, sees and describes it all with a coolness and a precision which is the opposite of detached. Turning her lack of inwardness with French, a language, after all, which she only started to learn at twenty-one, into a source of enormous strength, she shows that, for the born writer, no barriers are insurmountable.

L'analphabète is equally pared down and precise, but this story of exile and loss, of how, for the refugee, the country in which she eventually settles, however kind and well-meaning its inhabitants, will always be a poor and inadequate substitute for the country of one's birth, its language always an alien thing, however proficient she becomes in it—this is the story of so many people today that it is perhaps *the* story of our time, and Ágota Kristóf should perhaps be seen as our transnational bard.

Reading this brief and modest book you cannot help but be moved by the pain and suffering of her life, but even more, I think, be exhilarated by it as an example as well as an account of the extraordinary resilience of human beings. If the horrors we inflict on one another never cease to surprise and amaze, then let us not forget the goodness and strength of character we can also, sometimes, show. This book is a testimony to that.

Ágota Kristóf died in 2011, at the age of seventy-five.

GABRIEL JOSIPOVICI

TRANSLATOR'S NOTE

When I read *L'analphabète* (*The Illiterate*) a year ago, I felt I had to translate it. Here was the same voice as in *The Notebook*—sober and incisive. Each word—these French words acquired with such difficulty—said just what it meant to say, reduced by necessity to the purest, simplest expression, but also conveying irony and humor. It is a special kind of French—French written through the prism of Kristóf's native language, Hungarian. Kristóf has spoken about the frustration of writing in French, which she considers to be a "poor" language, which cannot express nuances that were available to her in Hungarian. Paradoxically, this lack contributes to the originality and the rarity of her language, and makes it particularly satisfying to translate. Entering her speech, we encounter the words as if they were being used for the first time, stripped of embellishment or metaphor or excess of meaning.

Ágota Kristóf, in *The Illiterate*, tells us, in eleven short chapters, what she wishes us to know about how she became a writer, through the vicissitudes of her life in Hungary and in Switzerland—and nothing more. In later years, it seems, she even regretted having published these short texts. Did she feel that they were unnecessary, or that they revealed too much? For my part, I am deeply grateful to her for having published them, because they speak to me as if I had always been waiting to read them.

And I am grateful to have the privilege of translating them for the first time into English, as a homage to one of the great writers of the twentieth century.

. . .

With grateful thanks to my sister Magda Bogin and my dear friend Gabriel Levin, who both read this translation with generous attention.

And my gratitude, as always, to my husband Alain, for the enthusiasm he shares with me for Ágota Kristóf's writing—and all the rest.

NINA BOGIN, AUGUST 2013

ÁGOTA KRISTÓF was born in Csikvánd, Hungary, in 1935. Aged twenty-one, Kristóf, her husband, and her four-month-old daughter fled the Soviet repression of the Hungarian Uprising to Austria and were resettled in Neuchâtel in French-speaking Switzerland. She began to learn the language of her adopted country while working in a factory making watches. Her first novel, *The Notebook* (1986), gained international recognition. Kristóf's other work includes plays and stories, as well as the novels *The Proof* (1988) and *The Third Lie* (1991), which complete the trilogy begun with *The Notebook*. She died in 2011.

NINA BOGIN, born in New York in 1952, has lived in France since 1976. She has published three acclaimed collections of poetry. Her previous translations include works on art, the cinema and literary criticism.

HELEN OYEYEMI was born in Nigeria and has written a dozen highly acclaimed books. She won the PEN Open Book Award.

GABRIEL JOSIPOVICI was born in Nice in 1940 and lived in Egypt from 1945 to 1956, when he came to Britain. He taught at the University of Sussex from 1963 to 1996. His work includes fiction, drama and criticism, and has been widely translated.